A THIN LINE BETWEEN LOVE AND Revenge

ERICA T. CAPRI

ERICA T. CAPRI

A THIN LINE BETWEEN LOVE AND REVENGE

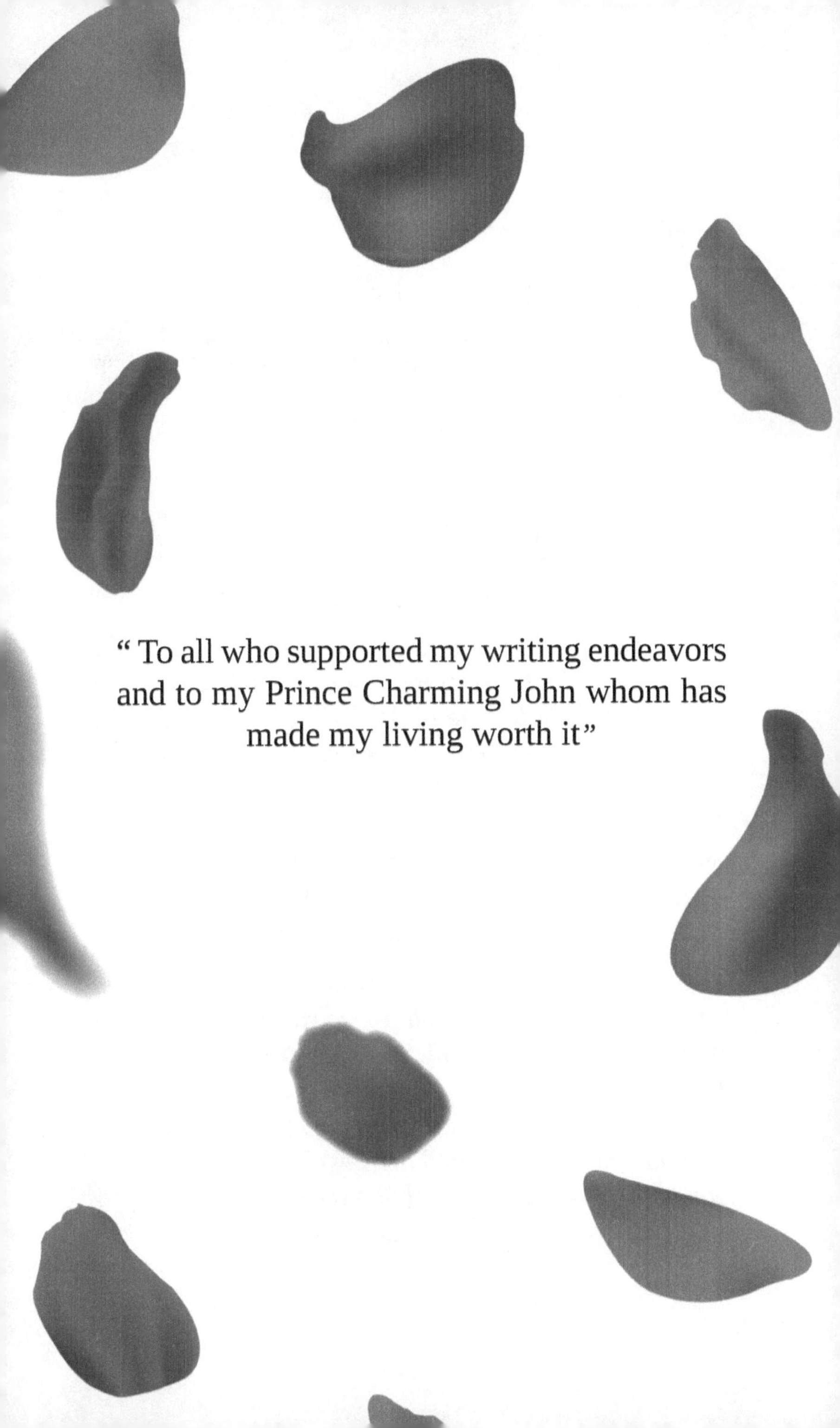

" To all who supported my writing endeavors and to my Prince Charming John whom has made my living worth it"

Prologue

I always wished I had children. I wished I could give birth like all the other women, but I couldn't. It was impossible for me until God proved to me that nothing was impossible with him. I was blessed with my beautiful daughter Destiny. She was the only child I had, so I loved and cherished her like my life depended on it; it did, because I knew baring another child would be hard, especially after what happened with my ex-husband. But God wasn't done with me.

Even though I didn't carry my second child, she was still my blood and flesh. When Kendra came, it felt like the world was finally complete for me. I felt like I could do whatever I wanted and however I wanted to do it. I was happy, so full of joy. I needed Kendra without knowing I needed her. I was glad Destiny had someone to share her childhood memories with, happy they had each other, and they came into each other's lives at a young age.

When Kendra first came into Destiny's life, I thought it was going to be hard for her to receive the little girl, but God gave Destiny so much love in her heart that she received Kendra with open arms, she received Kendra with a huge smile on her face, and a warm hug. The two girls practically became best friends on their first day, while Destiny took the role of an older sister, always holding Kendra, and trying to save Kendra from falling when she couldn't even walk perfectly herself.

It was why I was grateful to God. He always made things easy for me and my family. He always cleared my path and gave me a reason to laugh, no matter the situation.

Which was why I couldn't die young. Sure, the girls had people who would take care of them if anything happened to me, but it wasn't going to be the same as having their mother raise them. I could not die.

God didn't bless me with these two brown haired beauties for me to die and leave them behind for this cruel world to eat up. It would never happen, and God would never let that happen to me.

So sorry death, not today.

Chapter one

The bible says God will never give us a challenge we cannot handle. That verse in the bible has been my pillar for years, but as Isabella, who we all thought was dead, stood in front of me with a cocked gun pointed at me, and with a deadly smirk that spelled anger, I knew I had been given a challenge far greater than I am.

The first, among many things that crossed my mind, was how Isabella was still alive. Was it possible she faked her death, so she could escape going to jail for attempted murder? Many questions crossed my mind at that point, but I was scared to speak.

"I'm going to get back what belongs to me," Isabella smirked, her eyes glowed with anger and hatred. It was all directed toward me. I couldn't respond because of how scared I was.

"Lord, please save me," I prayed silently. Today was supposed to be the happiest day of my life, but I was standing on a thin line between life and death.

"USE YOUR WORDS!" I heard the command loud and clear in my heart. My words were my way out.

"Isabella?" I called out in a shaky voice; I couldn't even believe it was my voice. I was terrified because I had a lot of people I wanted to live for: my two daughters, my husband, my friends, and the women I preached to at conferences. That was my whole life, and Isabella was threatening to kill me. At some point, I thought she was a ghost because I remember vividly seeing a body lying lifeless in her bathtub. It was taken to the hospital where she was declared dead, so how is it possible that she is alive and holding a gun to me?

"In the flesh, baby, I'm sure you missed me dearly," Isabella smirked; her eyes had so much hatred and resentment toward me.

"I reported your death. I found you in that bathtub," I told her with confusion etched on my face like a tattoo.

"Oh, I know. I was there. Come closer, I'll let you in on a little secret," she smiled at me, motioning for me to come closer to her with the gun.

"I had to kill my twin sister for that show. The little brat was just like you, always claiming to be holier than everyone: Miss goody-two-shoes." Isabella was trying to act tough, but it was written all over her face just how much she regretted that one decision she made. It saddened me to think she would go that far for someone who wasn't even worth it.

"You are worse than Ethel was though," Isabella shook her head as if it would help shake away the memories of her sister and her bad decisions.

"You're still alive, and you think you can live a good life with Larry's wealth while I suffer. Larry never loved me; he pitied me. and He loved the fact that I could bear children. And even though I could bear children, he still used your egg, not mine. You were always first to Larry, and it disgusted me to no end because you didn't reciprocate his desperate feelings, which I yearned for. All I wanted was for Larry to love and acknowledge me, but what did he do? He decided to give you everything, including his wealth," Isabella spat.

"You know what? This is the last day for you, Kendall; any last words?" I could feel my breath ceasing already. I don't want to die, Lord.

"I shall not die but live to declare the words of the Lord," I found courage. I felt strong like I had someone backing me. I knew I wasn't alone, and I was not going to die.

"Okay, Kendall, let's see what the big man up there can do for you," Isabella cocked the gun, aiming the heavy black metal at me. I took a deep breath and closed my eyes. Immediately, the door to the room flew open, and then a shot was fired. A lot of things were happening at that moment. I could hear someone cry, and then I felt pressure on my body.

"Someone, anyone, call 911!!!" the muffled voice yelled.

It was then I felt it, the sharp pain on the lower part of my stomach. I kept looking straight ahead, where

Isabella once stood. I knew my faith would start to dwindle if I looked down at the assault she committed. Out of fear, Isabella shot me when someone opening the door, and once again, she escaped. The pain I felt was unexplainable. It started from my head down to my toes. As blood flowed out of me, it felt like life was pouring out of me. *I shall not die!* There were a lot of things I had to do and dying wasn't one of them.

Slowly, my legs gave up, and I could no longer stand on my own; I thought I was going to land on the floor with my headfirst, but fortunately, I felt a presence behind me, which wrapped its arms around me as my body made peace with the floor.

"Ken! Stay with me, baby, stay with me, you'll be fine," it was Connor's voice. I looked up to confirm he was really the one. With our eyes locked on each other, I couldn't help but feel more pain as I watched Connor cry. The fear in his eyes was evident; I wanted to tell him I would be fine, but the words were not coming out. It was almost like I lost my vocal cords. I couldn't say a thing; I could only look at him and wish he'd stop crying.

"Dear Lord, Kendall is yours; she's in your hands," those were the last words I heard Connor say before I lost consciousness.

Chapter two

When I opened my eyes, a bright light attacked my eyes, making it hard for me to see clearly at first. Slowly, my eyes adjusted to the light. I was finally able to see my surroundings. I was in an unfamiliar room, painted in white paint; it had white curtains shielding the windows, too. My first instinct was to get up and take a glass of water, but as I attempted to sit up, a wave of pain hit me hard in the head. The blow was so hard that I cried out in agony. I wasn't ready for the pain at all.

On cue, the door opened, and rushing in were Connor and an unfamiliar woman in a white lab coat with a stethoscope around her neck. She must be a doctor. Both of them ran toward me, but while the doctor ran the big monitor beside me, Connor ran directly to me, holding my hands in his as he kissed every corner of my face. The last time I saw him, he had tears of pain in his eyes as he looked down at me, but this time, he had tears of joy.

"Thank God you're awake! You have no idea how scary these past three weeks have been without you," Connor smiled at me. I smile back, pushing away every discomfort I felt in my body. I was alive. Just as I claimed, I didn't die.

"Sir, I'd like to run a few tests to see how she's doing. If you don't mind, can you kindly leave the room?" the doctor said with a small smile on her face. Connor looked from me to the doctor, and then he gave me an assuring smile before nodding his head. He placed a soft, tender kiss on my hand then stepped out of the room.

My life was a testimony. It was always going to be a testimony because bad things kept happening to me. These bad things were capable of ending my life, but God came through every time. He saved me and kept me alive.

Finally, the day came when I was to leave the hospital. The doctor who attended to me told me my recovery was unusual and she had never seen anything like it. Gunshot wounds typically don't heal quickly in the span of just three weeks. It was all God.

Connor was the true definition of a husband; he stayed by me throughout my stay in the hospital, sleeping in an uncomfortable cushion every night because he didn't want me to feel lonely. I hated that I had to spend the first four weeks of my marriage in the hospital, but it was beyond my control. There was nothing I could do about it. Through it all, though, Connor stayed by me, praying and tending to me. If I had doubts about my love for him before, all those doubts were out the window now.

For once, Connor had not spoken about my baby girls, which rubbed me the wrong way. How did they survive for four weeks without me? Destiny always claimed she was the older sister. Therefore, she could take care of herself. On the other hand, I was just getting to know Kendra, but then I got taken away from her like in an instant. Connor had not spoken about Scott and Carol either, and for some reason, he dismissed the topic immediately whenever I asked about them. He insisted I didn't have to worry about them, and I should only focus on my health and getting better.

I missed my girls dearly, so I cried a few times; it was just a lot for me to handle, but I was happy I would see my girls again. I would be able to hold them, kiss them, and tuck them into bed. I couldn't wait to get home, which was why, when Connor drove into the driveway, I had already opened the car's door to let myself out.

"Calm down, woman," Connor laughed. I didn't pay attention to him. I just wanted my girls. I was already out of the car before he turned off the ignition.

I power walked into the living room, only to find it empty; there was no welcome party of any kind. If anything, I was slightly disappointed.

"I think what you're looking for is behind the house." I felt Connor wrap his hand around my waist, pulling me to him.

"Welcome home, darling. I've missed having you around here so much," Connor whispered. I smiled and leaned into him.

"Come with me." Connor grabbed my hand and led me to the back of the house, where the house party I so desperately wanted was waiting for me.

"Mommy," my girls cried in unison, running to me. I knelt down and opened my arms wide to receive them. I missed them so much.

"Daddy said you went on a short trip," Destiny cried. The girls had gotten accustomed to calling Connor dad, and it was the sweetest thing. I turned to look at Connor, who gave me a sad smile.

"And he wouldn't let us go with him to see you," little Kendra sulked. I let out a small breath and hugged them to me. I

"You're well aware we're here too, right?" Scott laughed; he had his arms wide open for me. I smiled at him and Carol, who was standing beside him.

"It's okay to say you missed me, you know." I engulfed both of them in a hug. This was the family I wanted to live for, and I was so happy I got a second chance to be with them. Lord knows how dysfunctional they all would've been without me, especially my little girls.

"You need to tell us what happened. Connor said something about seeing Isabella before she escaped," Scott whispered.

"I thought she was dead?" Carol asked. I shook my head. I didn't want to relive that moment, but I had no choice; I would have to tell them eventually.

Chapter three

"Apparently, Isabella is, or rather was, a twin," I took a deep breath. The sun was setting, leaving an orange-yellow sky. I had successfully put my girls to sleep because I knew I was going to have a long night.

Connor, Scott, Carol, and I were seated in the living room after dinner. The topic of Isabella came up again, and I had questions to answer.

"What do you mean by 'was a twin'?" Scott asked me.

"The Isabella who died that day wasn't the real Isabella; it was her twin. Isabella killed her twin sister," saying the words felt heavy on my lips.

"Oh Lord have mercy," Carol put her hands above her chest.

"Why would she do that to her own blood?" Scott asked. He had his left hand under his chin while using his right hand for support.

"Well, Isabella said something about her sister acting 'holy.'" I guess her sister was trying to stop her from carrying out her horrible plans, so Isabella killed her," I explained.

"That's not a good reason to kill a sibling." Connor shook his head; I nodded in response. That was really a silly excuse. There must've been another reason why Isabella made the decision she did.

My heart was with Isabella, even though she tried to kill me. I couldn't stop picturing her as a stray animal that needed saving. Isabella was broken, and she knew she needed help, but she isn't the type of person to ask for help. She'd rather do things herself, with force.

"What about the police, though? They've been asking non-stop about you. Of course, Connor told them what Isabella looked like, but it was hard considering the fact that she was declared dead a year ago," Scott said. For some reason, I didn't want the police getting involved. I wanted to help Isabella God's way. If it meant giving some of Larry's properties to her, like the house and cars, I would do it just so she would be saved.

"I know that look, Ken. You're not thinking of helping her, are you?" Scott asked me. I let out a small laugh. Scott knew me all too well.

I took a deep breath and looked at all three of them.

"Look, I understand what Isabella did was wrong. Who knows if she wants to do it again? Still, I think she needs to be saved. I think she needs to know someone is there for her." Yes, I knew justice had to be served legally, with the police taking Isabella behind bars for attempted murder. Yet, deep down in my heart, I didn't want that to happen.

"No! I don't want you anywhere near that woman. I don't care what you plan to do, but if it's going to take you close to her, I forbid it. She can go join Larry where he is." Connor stood up. He was annoyed. I guess I had underrated how much he missed me.

"Babe, calm down. I'm just saying what has been in my heart. I think it's the will of God. Look, I strongly believe the same God who saved me from dying by her bullet will save me over and over again if it's my destiny to bring her to Christ," I spoke calmly.

"It's a scary thing, thinking about being that close to her again because no one knows what she might try to do again. Still, this is something I feel burdened to do. Ignoring it would mean I'm not grateful for the gift of life God granted me," I explained.

"I don't want to lose you: not now, not ever," Connor said, walking over to where I sat. He put me on his lap and wrapped his arms around me. I missed being in his arms this way. It was my safe haven. Connor made me feel like everything was possible.

"You're not going to lose me: not now, not ever," I smiled at him.

"Ehrm! We're still here, you know," Scott cleared his throat. I smiled at Scott's silliness. He was known for spoiling our mood, but we were already used to him and his silly jokes. So, we didn't mind.

"It's getting late; we should head home," Carol smiled at Connor and me.

"Thank you for coming; I really appreciate it," I smiled back at them.

"I think we've come too far for you to thank us for doing the bare minimum," Scott pouted. That was true, but I always felt better when I thanked people. It was a habit.

Scott said a prayer for me and then left the house with Carol.

"I'm so glad you're back. These past few weeks were hard on me. It felt like God had given me a test that was far above me. At some point, it felt like you were not going to wake up, but I knew I had to keep my faith if I ever wanted to see this beautiful smile of yours again. Also, your unfulfilled ministry of spreading love and positivity to people fueled my faith. It was the most challenging faith challenge I had ever experienced, but I'm glad we pulled through," Connor said, after which he started placing a trail of wet kisses down my neck.

Oh, dear lord, I had missed this too: the physical show of affection that Mr. Connor Collins was a pro at.

I let out small, stifled sounds, not caring one bit that my children were just upstairs.

"I love you, my dear," Connor whispered, biting the skin just underneath my ear lobe. My moans came out louder this time.

"Oh, Connor," I couldn't believe my own voice.

From behind me, I felt Connor's hands trail to my breasts, kneading them softly as he continued his assault on my neck. I loved what he was doing to me. I loved the way he made me feel. I loved everything about him. I loved this man. I loved him so much.

"Let's go upstairs," Connor's voice was deep and calm, and I knew why. From underneath me, I could feel his hard-on. I nodded my head immediately because I didn't want Destiny to wake up in the morning and see Connor and I laying naked on the couch. Not only would that be wrong, but it would also be embarrassing.

In one swift motion, I was in Connor's arms, my legs dangling from each side of him as he made his way to our matrimonial bedroom, which we hadn't used due to what happened to me.

Chapter four

It was a fine Friday afternoon, so Connor suggested a small picnic to celebrate my full recovery. The stitches in me had been taken out. Still, I couldn't engage in strenuous activities for the time being. I would admit, though, it was hard sitting around and doing nothing, not even combing my daughters' hairs. Connor did them all, without even so much as a complaint. I truly believed Connor was God sent; God brought him into my life to make up for my years of a bad marriage with Larry.

"Hey babe, are you okay? You're spacing out again," Connor smiled at me.

"Yes, I'm fine. I was just wondering what I did for God to bless me with such a great man like you," I smiled at him.

"You lived, struggled, and suffered, but you lived. You went through physical, emotional, and mental abuse, disguised as marriage, but yet you lived. You lived for me. That's what you did, and that's why you have me, so you never have to go through all of that again," Connor smiled and placed a chaste kiss on my lips. My heart was pounding against my rib cage, begging and crying to be let out. Was it possible to love a man as much as I loved Connor? It felt criminal, illegal, and just basically wrong. Yet, at the same time, it felt so right. I was giving him all the love I couldn't give Larry because Larry didn't deserve it.

I looked over to the park, keeping my eyes on Destiny and Kendra, who ran off to play with other children.

"Sometimes I wonder too," Connor went on, "what I did to deserve such a perfect woman, like you. Sometimes I feel I'm not worthy of being with you."

"My answer will not be any different from yours. You survived a toxic relationship for me. We were both broken by our partners, but God brought our broken parts together to make the perfect masterpiece," I smiled at him.

"You know, now that I think about it, you never went into detail about what really happened in your last relationship," I took up a slice of pizza, fitting half of it into my mouth.

"There's nothing to say. It was just bad overall. Nothing worth going into detail for," I noticed the way Connor dismissed the topic. Was there something going on I didn't know about? Maybe something he was trying to hide?

I shook my head immediately, forbidding the nasty thoughts I was accommodating. I didn't want to lose the trust I had in Connor. If I did, I would find it very difficult to trust anyone again. Connor was my pillar, and though he dismissed the topic about his ex-wife, I wanted to believe it was for a good cause, and there was nothing fishy going on.

I decided to forget about what had just happened and dwell on the fact that I loved my husband, no matter what.

"Isn't this just nice?" I heard a very familiar voice from behind us. I knew that voice all too well, and it was for none other than Isabella.

When Connor noticed she was the one, he quickly shifted, so he was crouched down in front of me. Isabella scoffed at Connor's action.

"I see you have refused to die," Isabella checked out her fingernails, not looking away from them once as she spoke.

"I told you I wasn't going to die," I dared to talk back.

"You brat! You should've just died! Why did you have to complicate everything?" Isabella cried.

Connor noticed her new change in emotion and pressed himself on me, making sure no part of my body was accessible to Isabella.

On cue, Destiny and Kendra came rushing toward us. When Kendra saw Isabella, she couldn't control the tears that started spilling from her eyes.

"She's bad, mommy," Kendra pointed at Isabella while tears flowed from her eyes like a waterfall. My heart broke for her. I pulled my girls to me immediately, hiding them behind Connor, just as I was doing.

"Shut your trap, you little dog! I lost my life because of you, and you have the bloody nerve to call me a bad mommy?" Isabella yelled. I covered Kendra's ears midway through Isabella's rant. The little child didn't have to hear all of those harsh words. She was not supposed to live with the trauma of Isabella's maltreatment.

"Don't you ever say those words to my daughter again!" Connor got up to face Isabella. I tried to pull him down, but he swatted my hand away.

"I'm not here for you; I only have business with Kendall over there," Isabella pointed at me.

"Well, she's my wife now, which means you have business with me! What happened to you was your fault. You thought you could go after a married man successfully? It's your punishment for thinking you were going to succeed; God got you. That's why you killed your sister, and now you're here, without anyone on your side. You're alone, with no one to call your own. It's your punishment," Connor's words were harsh, so harsh that I flinched. It was the first time I saw Connor this angry and annoyed. I never knew he had such side, since he was so cool, calm, and collected all the time.

"Don't you dare talk to me about God! I don't believe that crap you people believe in because it's a fraud! Do you know what I went through because of this 'God' of yours? Do you know what he did to me? And punishment, you say? That shows that this God of yours is really something? He took away my life, and now he thinks he has the right to punish me? What a sick joke!" Isabella yelled. I was confused. There were many things about Isabella that I didn't know about. She only let people see the things she wanted people to see: nothing more, nothing less.

"This God of yours took my parents from me and pushed me to a stupid Christian Orphanage home. My sister and I accepted our new status and found happiness by playing with other kids like us. We even loved it there, praying and thanking your God every day for the gift of life," Isabella scoffed.

"I believed what you believe in, but that went south when your God decided to send one of his workers to rape me when I was 17 years old! Tell me! Tell me how this ultimate father of yours could let a man, who taught us the word of God, rape a 17-year-old orphan!" Isabella yelled. My heart broke at her story. I couldn't keep the hurt I felt for Isabella in any longer. Tears rolled down my eyes uncontrollably as I watched her.

This was the very reason I had to help Isabella; she had lost her faith and thought of God as a fraud, which was very wrong in every way. I guess she thought the faith challenge she was given was above her.

"Do you want to know what shocks me the most?" Isabella asked. "That dickhead still preaches this so-called word of God. So, don't you ever try to mention any God near me!" Isabella yelled. She had tears in her eyes as she spoke.

Isabella then wiped her face with the sleeve of her black shirt and looked straight at me.

"I'm coming back for you, Ken. You're going to wish you died that day! I will do you dirty, just as you did to me!" Isabella threatened and ran away.

I could hear my heart beating rapidly. I was scared for Isabella and scared of Isabella.

I could understand every bit of what she went through because I went through something similar. I was in a place where I didn't trust God to be true for letting me get married to a man like Larry. I lost my faith and eventually lost myself, but there was light at the end of the tunnel for me, just as there's one at the tunnel for Isabella. It's only unfortunate that she is too far to see it. She didn't believe there would be a second chance for her, which broke my heart. This was what my ministry was about: bringing the lost souls, especially women, who had gone through severe trauma because of men. Isabella was a lost soul, and my mind was set on retrieving her. I was going to do it no matter how challenging. If God was going to use Isabella to test my faith, then I was ready for the challenge.

Chapter five

I couldn't sleep. I tossed and turned in my bed, but all I could think about were Isabella's words: her threats and her trauma. Wherever she was, she was hurting. She had no one to help her. No one was on her side. All she had were Connor's harsh words; he reminded her about being alone in the most horrible way.

I stood up from my bed and prayed about four times; yet I was restless. I kept thinking about Isabella. I got up from my bed and looked at Connor, who was sleeping soundly on the other side of the bed. He was gorgeous, even while sleeping.

I decided to take a stroll to the kitchen to get a glass of water, milk, or another liquid to lift my spirits. I wanted to feel better about myself so I could sleep.

When I got to the kitchen, I settled on a glass of cold water, which I nursed like a little baby, taking in small sips of it.

As I sipped on the water, I heard some weird sounds coming about from around the house. It almost sounded like someone was awake, and they were walking about the house.

"Who's there?" I grabbed a long wooden spatula as a weapon, just in case. The sounds ceased immediately, so I walked toward the direction of its origin to check what scared me so late in the night. There was nothing or no one in sight.

"Maybe this is the result of my overthinking," I said, laughing at myself.

"Holy Spirit, guide me," I paused and took in a deep breath. I walked back to the kitchen, dropped the spatula back from where I took it, and then carried my half glass of water with me.

While walking back to my room, I kept getting the urge to check up on Destiny and Kendra. The feeling was so strong in me, tugging at me like someone was pulling my nightwear.

"It's probably nothing." I shook my head but strolled over to their room to check up on them. Connor and I decided it was best to keep them in the same room because it would strengthen their relationship as sisters.

As I opened the door, fresh air from the window attacked me. Immediately, my heart sunk.

Why was their window opened? I lock it every night after singing a lullaby to them.

I switched on the light to check on them and discovered their beds were empty. There was not a single soul in the room. Before I could make a sound, I felt a sharp pain at the back of my head; someone had hit me. I didn't have the liberty to see who it was because I fell to the ground. Everything went black; I could see nothing. I was in a very dark place, and slowly, I lost all consciousness.

Chapter six

The pain I felt in the back of my head brought me to consciousness. I slowly opened my eyes, but it was too bright for me. The light made it almost impossible to see with my eyes scrunched close.

When my eyes finally got accustomed to the light, I let my eyes wander about without trying to sit up. I felt the weakness of my body in the position I was in. I didn't want to suffer again. So, I stayed still.

The familiar walls, curtains, and the beeping sounds of the monitor beside me was enough to tell me where I was. I was in the hospital again, waking up to soreness all over my body.

"Call the doctor! I think she's up." I knew his voice all too well; it was Scott. From his voice, I could tell just how tired and worried he had been.

"Ken, oh thank God, Ken," Carol said as she ran to my side, holding my hands in hers.

"What's wrong? How did I get here?" I asked her. I saw the fear in Carol's eyes.

"Do you know who I am, Ken?" She asked, waving her hands in my face. I smiled slightly, nodding my head the best I could while lying down.

"What's my name?" Scott ran to me.

"Scott," I said, letting out a breath.

"Oh, thank God. You had us scared for a second. We thought you lost your memory or something," Scott said, placed his hand on his chest.

"Do you not remember what happened to you?" Carol asked. I looked from Carol to her husband, trying to recall what happened to me. What caused this predicament of being in the hospital again?

"We believe you were hit with something heavy on the back of your head. Luckily, Connor found you, but you were out by then," Scott explained.

Oh, dear Lord, Connor.

Then, it hit me. My children were taken from our home in the middle of the night, and I could not do anything to save them!

"Destiny! Kendra!" I widened my eyes in disbelief as the thought of my children being in an unknown location consumed me. They must be scared to death. Oh, poor Kendra.

Almost immediately, I hopped out of bed, pushing Scott and Carol aside as they both tried to stop me from moving. I ignored the pain I felt in my body as I made my way out of the room. My children were taken away from their home, where they were supposed to feel safe the most. How could I think of myself and my pain when my girls were going through worse pain?

"Dear Lord Jesus, I put those beautiful girls into your hands. Nothing bad can happen to them," I prayed as I made my way out of the hospital building, ignoring all the calls for me to stop. I could not.

I knew this was a test from God, but I couldn't help but feel it was a little bit unfair to put my girls amid everything, especially when Isabella had a murderous intent. I shook my head, trying to eliminate the negative thoughts from my head.

God had saved me from an abusive marriage, gave me two daughters, and gave me a man who cherished me more than anything. God gave me a second chance at life, so who was I to think such thoughts? I decided to save Isabella. If delivering my girls into Isabella's hands was a way to bring Isabella into God's hands, then I knew for a certain my girls were going to be okay. I was panicking for no reason.

I stood barefoot in a hospital gown in the middle of a parking lot, looking for something to transport me elsewhere. I needed to find Connor to make sure he wasn't doing the wrong things.

"Ken!" Scott's voice stopped me. I turned to the hospital entrance, watching him as he ran toward me with Carol behind him.

"If you could run that fast this whole time, you should've become an athlete," Scott scolded.

"Where do you think you're going in the middle of the night, dressed like a psychiatric patient with no shoes on," he continued. Carol was too out of breath to talk.

"I must find Connor," I told him.

"You don't even know where he is," Carol yelled. It was the first time Carol raised her voice at me, but I couldn't blame her. I understood her frustration. If I were in her shoes, I'd feel even more frustrated than the both of them combined.

"You need rest, Ken. Connor is fine. You don't have to worry," she lowered her voice.

"He went to report the situation at the police station, and he said he'd meet us here afterward," Carol added.

"I need to stop him from reporting the kidnap, so I can save Isabella" I ran my fingers through my hair. Scott and Carol had disbelief etched on their faces.

"Ken, I know you think this is the will of God, but Isabella should be arrested," Carol spoke softly like I was a kindergarten student.

"I need to get changed, but after that, you'll take me to Connor. I don't want him to worry about me," I told them.

Scott and Carol shared a look and nodded. They led me back into the hospital, where I was given the clothes I came in with. As I dressed up, my mind stayed focused on Connor and what he might have been feeling. I hated the thought of him being frustrated; it frustrated me.

"You ready?" Scott asked me after I came out of the hospital room, fully dressed in my nightwear. I looked normal enough, except for the big bandage wrapped around my head.

Scott and Carol led me to their car, and we went to the police station. The time was 3:26 a.m., which meant the streets were empty, and everywhere seemed calm. As the wind from the windows rolled down hit my face, it washed away all the worries I had felt when I woke up because I knew God was going to keep my girls alive, just like he had for me.

Chapter seven

When Connor saw me, he ran to me immediately, hugging me close to him. It was his way of telling me everything was going to be okay, and I believed him. I did not doubt him because I had a firm conviction in my spirit that we would come out victorious.

"You could've stayed at the hospital. I'm done here anyway," Connor had his forehead pressed against mine as he spoke.

"I wanted to see you," I whispered to him. He let out a small laugh.

Connor looked as frustrated as I had imagined he would be. He wasn't even my daughters' real father, but his love for them was pure and genuine. It surprised me sometimes when I thought about it. Connor was really the perfect man.

He had on different types of slippers on his feet, and his hair was scattered all over the place. He looked tired, mostly because he was sleeping when everything happened. I couldn't even imagine what it might have been like for him to see me collapsed on the floor while the children's room was empty.

"I was so scared. I didn't even know how to pray," Conner said, interlocking our hands.

"Always find the words to talk to God!" I reprimanded. Connor laughed and placed a soft kiss on my forehead.

"Let's get out of here. We'll have to come back here later anyway; they'll need your statement." Connor smiled. I nodded and let my husband lead me out of the almost empty police station to his car. "I can't thank you guys enough for looking after her," Connor said as he leaned into Scott's rolled-down car window to talk to them.

"No need to thank us, it's our duty to take care of one another." Scott hit the steering wheel lightly, smiling at us.

"Good night. God bless you," I said, waving at them as they rolled out of the police station's parking lot.

"Let's get out of here." Connor led me to his car, and we drove home in comfortable silence. When we got home, we prayed, and when my head hit my pillow, I fell into a deep sleep, even though the worst thing had happened to me earlier.

I woke up to the sound of my phone ringing loudly in my ears. It was an unknown caller.

"Hello?" I said into my speaker. Connor wasn't in bed beside me, I noticed. He probably went to make breakfast.

"If it isn't the lady who is second to Jesus! You always find a way to stay alive, don't you?" Isabella laughed.

"Isabella! Where are my children?" I was on full-alert mode now; all traces of sleep were cleared from my eyes. My children are very important to me, so I knew the hell I had to walk through to get them. I was not going to let her walk over them like that.

"Whoever said I took your kids?" Isabella laughed. I was quiet because I didn't trust her.

"Okay, okay, I did take your kids. And all you have to do to get them is to bring the documents of everything Larry left behind," Isabella said. It still shocked me to think Isabella would kidnap my girls because of what Larry left behind.

"Fine! I'll bring them. Where do we meet?" I asked immediately. Isabella said she would text me the location of the place we'd meet.

I hung up and hit the shower, praying as I moved about.

I got dressed and went downstairs to the kitchen. Connor was still nowhere to be found. He probably went to get some groceries, right?

I took a glass of water and ran back to my room, fishing for anything with Larry's name on it. I didn't want to be associated with either of them anymore; they belonged to each other. They deserved each other.

In my head, I could hear Larry's pleas for me to ignore Isabella's ploy to get hold of his properties, but what was Larry's riches to me if I didn't have my kids? It was nothing. Nothing mattered to me more than them, so I was ready to give up whatever it took to get them back.

When I found all the documents, I grabbed my phone to see Isabella had sent the location. I immediately called Scott and Carol, telling them about mine and Isabella's plans, and how I couldn't find Connor after futile attempts to reach him on call.

Scott and Carol said they'd pray for me from home, as they didn't want to tag along and make Isabella annoyed. It made sense; I thanked them and hung up.

Isabella had told me to meet her at a warehouse by 12:00 p.m. sharp. It was 10:36 p.m., so I started driving. I called Connor to leave him a voice message, so he'd know how to find me.

The warehouse was approximately forty-five minutes away from where we lived, so I was able to pray for forty-five minutes, all the way to the warehouse. When I got to the warehouse, I called Isabella, and she sent a man dressed in a black outfit to come and get me.

"Where are my children?" I asked her. She smiled at me like she was daring me to test her.

"Not even a hi, or hello?" She asked me, waving her hands toward me. I rolled my eyes but kept my mouth shut.

"Bring the brats," Isabella yelled, and then there was movement. Many men dressed in black, similar to the man who came to get me, ran about like they were looking for something. Then, I heard screams. My girls were screaming for help.

"You know, this was easy. It makes me think you have something else planned. Do you have the police outside?" Isabella asked me. I shook my head.

"What about that fine husband of yours? There's someone I'd like him to meet." Isabella rubbed her palms together, then rubbed her hands across the long black coat she had on.

"I just want my children," I said, throwing the documents in my hands across the floor from her.

"You're feisty, and I like it," Isabella laughed, and her goons joined her.

Soon, two men dressed in black brought my children out front, making them face me while backing Isabella.

"I'm going to kill you, for real this time, Kendall," Isabella said as she pulled out a gun.

"I'm not going to die. I shall not die! But live and declare the works of the Lord to the full," I proclaimed.

"Really?" Isabella smiled. She cocked her gun, but instead of pointing it at me, she had it pointed at Kendra's head.

"Isabella!"

Chapter eight

I jolted up with force, placing my right hand in my chest as I recalled the horrible thing that just happened, which, thankfully, was a dream.

I wasn't at ease, though, because I knew my dreams were hardly far from reality.

I recalled the dream I had about Kendra while I was sleeping on the airplane last year; it turned out to be true. That was my type of prophetic ministry, but I only saw details about my life or things linked to me.

Isabella had murderous intentions. She was going to kill my children if given the opportunity. I could feel so much anger and hatred radiating from her through the dream.

I looked over at the other side of the bed; Connor

was sleeping soundly like a baby, as usual. So, I pushed the duvet we shared away from me, got out of the bed, and got on my knees. I put my hands together and started praying.

If there was anything I could do for my children, it was to pray for them. I had no idea what they were going through. I couldn't make sure they had eaten or not. There was no way I could know if they were sick. It hadn't even been 24 hours since they were taken away from their rooms, but it felt like ages. I missed my children. I missed my girls so much.

I think my prayers caught Connor's attention because he stirred a few times in his sleep before finally waking up. I locked eyes with him for a second and continued my prayers, and soon, he was beside me, holding my hands in his as we prayed together. We prayed away the spirit of death from our children.

An hour later, we were done with our prayers, and my phone rang loudly. It was an unknown caller, just like in my dream.

I took in a deep breath while looking at Connor; his approving nod gave me more strength, and I picked up the call. I knew it was Isabella without having to hear her speak.

"Oh, Kendall," Isabella moaned.

"You must be a cat with nine lives," Isabella laughed at her lame attempt at a joke.

"My kids, Isabella," I said, going straight to the point. The lives of my innocent children were at stake here. I couldn't risk it by prolonging my talk with her for no reason.

"I didn't even tell you I took them. I mean, I did, but how did you know?" She laughed.

"Don't bother answering that; you'd probably hit me with something about God. I have a proposition," she said. From the way she talked, I knew she was smiling.

"I have all of Larry's things ready. That's what you want, right?" I asked her.

She was quiet for a while. I guess she did not expect me to talk about Larry's property, but apart from the dream I had, it was self-evident she was only after Larry's stuff. She tried to kill Larry because he had everything handed over to me.

"You're smart, aren't you, Kendall?" Isabella let out strained laughter.

"I'll send you a location. And just so I remind you, in situations like this, you don't bring the police with you, or you lose your lovely girls," Isabella said, trying to hold back her giggles.

"Oh, and also bring your hot husband with you. There's someone I'd like him to meet: his old friend," Isabella said before she hung up.

Old friend? I recalled my dream and how Isabella had said something about an old friend. Who was this old friend? What did Connor have to do with someone who knew Isabella?

I let my phone escape from my hand as I sighed. "What was wrong, dear Lord?"

"Did you have a bad dream? What's wrong?" Connor hit me with questions. I had the answers to his questions, but for some reason, I kept my eyes on him while my mind was roaming about, seeking answers.

"Babe!" Connor shook me. I jumped and shook my head. Connor was talking to me, but I couldn't hear or understand him.

"Yes?"

"Tell me what happened," Connor urged.

"I had a dream last night about everything that just happened; Isabella calling me and asking me to bring the documents for all of Larry's properties. When I got to the location, something weird happened, though. There were men dressed in black everywhere, and Isabella pointed a gun at Kendra's head, claiming she was going to kill my precious little child. Then, Isabella asked about you in my dream, saying she had someone she wanted you to meet, like an old friend. I didn't pay much attention to that because I thought it was unnecessary, but she just said the same thing now. She asked that you come with me," I explained to him.

"An old friend?" Connor asked. I nodded my head, hoping for some answer, but I got nothing from him.

"That's news to me," Connor said. His aura had changed from "nice and friendly" to "back off." I nodded my head and went to find Larry's documents.

I wanted to press on and ask more questions, but I didn't have anything to fall back to, only that Isabella claimed there's someone she'd like him to meet. There was not much to it, but I knew I had to stop. My children were more important to me than some reunion party between Connor and his old friend. So, I focused on looking for the documents.

Chapter nine

"Everything will be fine," Connor said as he placed his hands on my shoulder and tried to calm me down. We had arrived at the location Isabella sent. The environment looked forgotten and tattered with dirt everywhere, steel and woods lying helplessly on the ground.

I nodded my head, took in a deep breath, and we climbed out of the car.

There was a man, dressed in all black. He had on black denim trousers, a black jacket, a black mask, and a black face cap. I was amazed at the details my dream offered; almost everything was the same and going in line with what I had seen.

On instinct, Connor pushed me behind him as a way of trying to protect me from the man.

"Follow me," The man said and turned around, going through a small door that I hadn't noticed when we arrived. So, it was like a long-forgotten warehouse.

What's the issue with kidnappers and warehouses anyway?

Connor grabbed my hand, interlocked our fingers real tight, adjusted Larry's documents in his other hand, securing them under his armpit, then we followed the man.

The house barely had any light entering it, and it was 4:27 p.m. There were streaks of light that found their way into the warehouse, but it was minor. I didn't notice any windows, almost like the place had none.

Connor's grip on my hand tightened even more, so much that I lost my blood circulation on the hand.

"Connor, it hurts," I whispered to him. He turned to me, and I gave him a small smile, looking from him to our intertwined hands, so he knew what I was talking about.

"Sorry," he released my hand, but he made sure I was standing very close to him.

"Kendall!" I heard someone call my name. It sounded like Isabella, but I wasn't so sure because the person had called my name softly, something Isabella had never done before. Connor and I locked eyes. He looked just as confused as I was.

"Kendall," the person called my name again, followed by sniffs. Was she crying?

The voice sounded closer to us than the first time the person had called. What was going on? With the help of the tiny light streaks, Connor and I found our way into the warehouse.

"Isabella? Is that you?" I called out. Where had the man who ushered us in gone? I felt like we were the only ones in the warehouse. I was confused as to what had happened and why this person sounded like they were crying.

"Will your God accept me even after everything I've done?" The voice asked. I took a few more steps forward, and I was standing before Isabella. She looked beaten up and tired. Her clothes and hair were messy.

"He'll accept you, Isabella! What happened?" I ran to her.

"Dead children. I see dead children everywhere, and Ether is leading them. Please make it stop," she cried.

"I'm scared," she added. I held Isabella in my arms and rocked her slightly.

"I've tried to kill you twice. I tried to kill your children and harm your marriage; yet, here you are, holding me," Isabella said. I closed my eyes and took in a deep breath.

"Yes, you did all those things, but for some reason, my heart kept going out to you. I wanted to help you," I explained to her. Isabella had tears in her eyes. She must've seen horrible images all night because the eye bags under her eyes were large.

When I woke up with the urge to pray for my children, I had no idea it was the way God would deliver Isabella into my hands, literally. God arrested her, and it was time for her to be saved.

"It has never been my intention to go this far. I just wanted to get over Larry and find a way to heal from killing my sister, but they kept pushing me. They kept urging me to deal with you," Isabella's voice was tiny. Who was "they"? Had Isabella been working with people?

No wonder I noticed two people in the house the day Destiny and Kendra were taken. "What had we done to these people that they decided to make my family bleed this way?"

"While my target was you, their target was Connor," Isabella revealed. Connor? Why Connor? I thought hard about how Isabella said she wanted to reunite Connor with an old friend. She was referring to these people who had made her do horrible things to my family and me?

"Where are they now, Isabella?" I asked her.

"They left shortly before y'all arrived," Isabella said.

"We had a big misunderstanding, and they left with threats to kill me even," Isabella explained. So, God had caused confusion in the camp of the enemy and delivered them into our hands.

"Isabella, the man who brought us in, where is he?" I asked.

"There was no man. I was the one who ushered both of you in," Isabella said.

"Kendall, I'm sorry. I don't even want Larry's properties. It'll only bring back bad memories, and I want to start afresh," Isabella cried. This God was and is wonderful. Everything was working in my favor, nice and simple.

"Kendall? I've found the girls!" Connor's bright voice made me smile.

"Let's get out of here?" I asked Isabella. She nodded her head, and I helped her up, leading her out of the warehouse and to the car.

There was nothing better than trusting in God. In one day, God had delivered my oppressor into my hands, scattered the plans they had, and made sure nothing bad happened to me or my family.

When Connor came out of the warehouse with Destiny and Kendra, both of them on each side of him, I ran to them immediately and hugged them to me.

"I missed you, momma," Destiny cried. While Kendra just held me tight without saying a word. I missed them so much, my girls. They looked clean, without any scratches on their bodies.

"What happened?" Connor asked, looking from Isabella, who had leaned on the car for support, to me.

"I'll explain later, let's get out of here."

Chapter ten

"Kendall! We'll be late!" Connor called.

"Give me a minute!" I yelled back at him. I was in our room, trying to apply some lipstick, while he was downstairs with the children, waiting for me.

It had officially been two weeks since the whole kidnap situation, and two weeks since Isabella was saved, even though she had to serve time in prison because of her crimes.

To celebrate our drama-free life, Connor suggested a family dinner with Scott and Carol. It was the perfect plan, but we were about to be late. I kept applying different lipstick shades on my lips because I couldn't find the perfect shade.

"Oh, whatever!" I threw the red lipstick I was applying across the table, grabbed my purse, and ran down the stairs to meet with my family.

Connor had offered to get the girls dressed while I got myself ready. That was the perfect plan, considering how much time I wasted to get prepared.

"You look beautiful, mommy." Kendra smiled shyly at me.

"And so do you, both of you." I hugged my girls.

"I don't think I like how you girls beat me to compliment mommy," Connor joked, feigning anger.

"Well, what did you expect them to do when all you did was stare at me, without saying a word," I said, rolling my eyes at Connor.

Connor pulled me to him, placing his hands on the small of my back. He inhaled my neck before smiling at me.

"You look wonderful, my love," he said and placed his lips on mine. At that moment, it felt like everything had faded into the background, and it was just us. The feeling was fleeting as I soon realized it wasn't just us. The girls were watching. I pushed Connor away from me softly, telling him with my eyes that the girls were watching.

"You look very handsome, my love," I smiled at him.

"Your compliment is late. I'm not accepting it," Connor joked, and I laughed.

We led the girls out of the house, making sure to firmly lock the doors, then we headed on our way.

Scott and Carol were already at the restaurant Connor picked, waiting patiently for us.

"Oh my God, you guys should've called," I told them.

"Or even come to the house first," Connor added.

"No, it's okay, you guys are here anyway," Carol smiled.

"You guys look good," Carol smiled.

"Aunt Carol!" Destiny ran to Carol, while Kendra ran to Scott. I watched the way the couple played with my kids; they were such good people, and no doubt good parents. They just had to produce their offspring.

I said a short silent prayer on their behalf, asking God to give them children. They had been trying to get kids for a while now.

Connor and I took our respective seats and looked through the menu. Connor ended up ordering a family buffet for us, and everyone dug in while talking about the horrors we had been through in the past few weeks and laughing over it like it was nothing.

We were so deep in our conversation that we didn't notice the lady standing at the foot of our table glaring at us. I was the one who noticed her first. She had thick, long wavy hair that flowed beautifully at her back. She had on a short back gown and black stilettos. Overall, she looked beautiful.

"Can I help you?" I asked her. She ignored me, and she kept her eyes trained on something, no, not something, someone: Connor.

"It's been a long time, Connor," she smiled at him.

Chapter eleven

"It's been a long time, Connor," she smiled at Connor with her arms folded. She had the look of mockery on her face as she kept her eyes trained on Connor.

Connor was frozen in his spot. He couldn't move or talk; he kept his eyes trained on the woman. What was going on? And since when was Connor afraid of talking to people? Who is she?

"Connor?" I called my husband, placing my hands on his to get his attention. Connor responded to me, but his eyes were still trained on her.

"I'm sorry, who are you?" I got fed up and asked the lady. She looked like she was enjoying herself way too much for my liking. She was having fun seeing the way Connor was responding to her, and that was annoying as it was scary.

"Why don't you ask Connor here?" She giggled.

"From the look of things, I'm not sure my husband wants to talk to or see you. As you can see, we're having family time, so if you don't mind, please leave," I smiled sweetly at the lady.

The lady laughed, like really laughed.

"You know, I heard about you but for some reason, I didn't take you seriously," her words were accompanied by anger.

"Well, you heard my wife. We're having family time, and you're disturbing us," Connor finally found his words. I turned to him immediately, smiling at him.

"Connor, this isn't the best time to brag about your wife and you. I'll forgive you this time. You have to come and see me. It's not a threat or a suggestion, it's an order unless of course, you want bad things to keep happening to you and your family," she said still smiling.

"Rose, listen to me and listen well; I'm not a toy or a puppet you can command whenever you want. I don't have anything to discuss with you. So, I'd prefer if you never came anywhere close to me or my family," Connor said through gritted teeth. He sounded dangerous like he wasn't the sweet guy I met on a plane a year ago. He sounded mean, like the type of mean you'd only see on television.

On instinct, I leaned over to Destiny and Kendra, holding their hands to let them know mommy was there with them no matter what. Kendra wrapped both hands around mine. She was scared of this Rose lady almost as if she had seen the woman somewhere; Destiny had the same expression on her face too. Had they seen her before? I wondered.

"Connor, we have to go," I said. If my children were not comfortable, there was no need to have family time. The night had been ruined, and there was nothing anyone could do to revive it unless we went home.

Connor and Rose were having a staring competition, no one wanting to back down first.

"Connor!" my voice was a bit louder than usual, but it did the trick. Connor looked at me with an apologetic look in his eyes; he hooked his left hand into mine, then looked back at Rose.

I had forgotten about Carol and Scott. They just sat on their respective seats, watching everything unfold. I was too angry and embarrassed to care.

"This is not the end, Connor, or should I call you Spax?" Rose laughed as she made her way out of the restaurant.

Spax? What was that? Connor's middle name wasn't Spax; it was Josiah, so why would she call him Spax?

I turned to Connor immediately. I needed answers to all the questions I had in mind.

"Before you say anything, let's at least get home and tuck the girls in first," Connor pleaded.

I relaxed a bit, then nodded my head. The girls looked shaken so putting them first was only fitting.

"I'm sorry guys for this trash dinner," I said to Scott and Carol, who looked very uncomfortable. They had just witnessed something they weren't supposed to with me.

I carried Kendra in my arms while Connor carried Destiny, then we left the restaurant. The whole family dinner was ruined by Rose; what was her deal anyway?

When we got home, I couldn't shake off the feeling that Connor was avoiding me or at least trying to avoid me. After tucking the girls into bed, Connor dashed out of their room, claiming he had to go to the bathroom. When he finally came out, he hurried to the kitchen, claiming he was hungry. He apparently wanted to whip up something small to eat. I didn't say a word to him; instead, I just nodded my head.

My mind was feeding a lot of lies, and Connor wasn't making it any better. What was it he was hiding? How bad was it? Why is it making him act cowardly? I loved and trusted Connor, but his behavior was alarming — almost like he wasn't the same person.

In just a few hours, I had seen two sides to Connor, which I had never seen in my entire life. These were sides I didn't think were possible to see because I didn't believe they were a part of Connor. Everything felt foreign to me.

While waiting for Connor in our room, I decided to lay down, turning my back to the door. A few minutes later, the door flew open, and Connor walked in. He probably thought I was sleeping, so he let out a sigh and said the words: "Thank God she's asleep."

I didn't know how to respond to his statement. And for some reason, I couldn't move. I just laid there. I was frozen in place, unable to decode what was happening.

I closed my eyes tight, saying a small prayer to God to help me out in the situation I just found myself in.

I didn't want to think anything bad about Connor. He didn't deserve that. He had been nothing but the sweetest husband on the planet. Even though everything happening lately was shady, I could only trust him. His words are the only things that matter to me If he was hiding anything from me, then that's his problem. I wouldn't ask because if he wanted to tell me, he wouldn't go through all these lengths to avoid telling me.

God, please help me stay true to my words.

Chapter twelve

If I thought last night was bad, then I sure wasn't ready for today. I had woken up as early as I could to get the girls ready for school, but to my surprise, Connor woke up before me and was already getting the girls ready for school. Normally, anyone would find his actions nice and beautiful, but that was not the case for me. I knew he was only doing it so he could avoid me.

God help me!

I prayed to God. I asked him for some peace of mind to keep me from making a billion of inquires in my head. Connor was a brave man, which was one of the reasons why I loved him, but he was chickening out and acting really scared of me. He was behaving as though I had the power to do something bad to him; I didn't, so I didn't understand his behavior at all.

"I see you're up. Good morning baby," I forced a smile on my face as I walked to him to give him a peck on his cheek.

"Mommy! Good morning, mommy," Destiny ran to me and Kendra followed. I smiled at my girls as I knelt to receive them.

"How did you sleep?" I asked them.

"I slept good mommy," they replied at the same time. I nodded my head and gave them pecks on their foreheads.

I looked up at Connor, who was already looking down at me. I flashed him a smile and got up.

"I'm going to make breakfast for them," I said and left their room.

I could feel how uncomfortable Connor was; it was almost physical. It didn't have to be like this if only he'd tell me what Rose wanted.

I took a deep breath, took out pancake mix, and mixed it quickly. When I was done making breakfast, Destiny and Kendra came running into the kitchen. I smiled at them.

"Where's daddy?" I asked my girls.

"He went back to your room," Destiny answered as she put a chunk of pancake into her mouth.

Throughout the whole morning, up until Connor left the house to work, we didn't lock eyes. Everything was becoming too much for me. I trusted Connor, not only as a person, but as someone who God brought into my life to make everything easier for me. But right now, I could feel my trust in him shaking. Different ideas were popping into my mind, and I couldn't block them out because Connor had not told me what to believe. I was conflicted and hurt.

When it was time to get the girls from school, I packed up a sleepover bag for them, so they'd stay at Scott and Carol's place. The environment in the house was not conducive for them at all.

I picked up the girls from school and called Carol, letting her know I was bringing the girls to them. Carol was ecstatic. She loved the children so much. Since she didn't have children of her own, Destiny and Kendra were like her children too.

"Is something wrong, Ken? You don't look so good," Carol asked. We had gotten to her house already. The girls were outside playing, while Carol, Scott, and I were in the living room.

"No, not at all. And I don't know what to do or how to go about it," I sighed.

"Oh Ken," Carol took my hands in hers.

"Is this about dinner last night?" Scott asked. I took a deep breath and nodded.

"Connor still hasn't come clean about Rose, and he's been acting strange. His behaviors are feeding me ungodly thoughts, and I can't stop them. I don't know what to believe," I let it out.

"What did he do?" Carol asked. I told them how Connor had been avoiding me. All these things were embarrassing to talk about, but I couldn't help it. I needed help.

"You should find a way to talk to him no matter what," Carol said.

"Yes, well, I've been trying, but he's not giving me the attention or the space to talk to him. I don't even know what to do anymore," I told her.

"Do you want me to talk to him?" Scott asked me.

"No." If Connor couldn't talk to me, there was no way he'd talk to Scott. I just knew it.

"That's why I brought the girls here. I'll just have to find a way to talk to him," I said, thinking of ways I could get Connor to talk to me.

"I pray y'all get past this soon," Scott said, and Carol nodded. I pray we get past it soon too.

A lot of stuff had happened to us in a short while, and if anything, we were supposed to be closer than ever. I mean I almost lost my life, and then my children. So this really was not the time to harbor hate, anger, or problems.

"Take care of my girls for me," I smiled at them, and they nodded. I waved my girls goodbye and walked to my car.

I drove home with a lot of thoughts flying about in my head. So, I turned off the car, held the steering wheel tight, and prayed.

The hurt I was feeling was too much to handle, and I couldn't imagine seeing Connor in a different light. I needed God's guidance to help me through this trial and temptation. So, I prayed and cried to God.

When I was done praying, I got out of my car,

only to see the last person I wanted to see, staring with amusement on her face.

"You've got to be kidding me," Rose laughed.

"Were you sleeping in your car?" She added. I rolled my eyes at her, looking away from her and to my house.

"What are you doing here?" I asked her.

"I'm here to see you, Kendall. I'm sure you've been expecting me, but you won't admit it," she smiled.

"State your course," my words were firm.

"Oh, sweet poor Kendall."

Chapter thirteen

"Oh, sweet poor Kendall," Rose said in a sulky tone, then she burst out in laughter.

"I'll have you know I'm not the type of person you should mess with, and it'll do you a lot of good if you drop that attitude of yours. I'm pretty dangerous you see," she said, and I knew she was serious.

"I'm not the person you should mess with either," I told her.

"Say whatever you have to say and be on your way." I gave her a small smile. Rose laughed.

"Connor," she called, and my eyes shot open.

"You have no idea who that man is, and what he's capable of," Rose smiled.

"From the look on your face, I'm guessing he hasn't told you anything about me yet. I wonder why that is.

Maybe he doesn't trust you as much as you think he does. He's hiding the biggest part of his life from you," she said as she adjusted the black blazer she had on.

"Connor may pretend to be a good man to you, but trust me, he's horrible. He has killed a lot of people, broken a lot of families, and thrown away destinies. Who knows, he might just be doing the same with you," Rose sized me from head to toe.

"Connor would never!" I spat. God help me.

"Okay, let me ask you this, did he ever tell you about his ex-wife and what happened between them?" She asked.

"He told me he was in a toxic marriage," I replied to her.

"Of course he did. Did he also tell you that he was the toxic one in the relationship? Did he tell you why I did what I did? What about the real reason we had to end it?" Rose was getting angry. So, she was his ex-wife?

"That's the thing with Connor: he deceives people, ruins them, and leaves them for good. I'm sorry to say, but my real reason for coming here is to take Connor back to where he belongs!" Rose said.

"That's the Connor you married. The man I married is God-fearing, and he's never done such a thing to anyone. Maybe you're saying all these things because of sheer jealousy, but I've seen what jealousy can do to a woman. It's not pretty at all," I told her.

"Are you referring to Isabella? She's lucky I didn't end her life after what she did to me," Rose spat. So,

Rose knew Isabella too? This was news to me. I never knew Isabella was in contact with Rose.

"Isabella told me she was going to kill you so I could get my man back, but she couldn't. Thanks to her, I found him, and that was the only reason why I didn't put a bullet through her skull." Rose smiled.

"Who exactly are you?" I asked Rose. I was confused.

"Connor's wife, and that's all you have to know," Rose smiled.

"I want to stay and chat with you Kendall, but I have other engagements. Think about everything I told you, and we'll talk again sometime soon," Rose said as she smiled at me and then disappeared.

This was almost the same thing that happened with Isabella. It was happening again. History was repeating itself in the worst way, and I was not ready for it at all.

What do I do, Lord?

I sighed and walked into the house. Thank God I sent the girls to Scott and Carol's place. What would I have done if they picked up that there was something wrong between Connor and me?

I hurried up to my room, took a warm shower, and laid on the bed. I couldn't move. I couldn't function. I could only think about Rose and what she said to me.

A few hours later, I woke up to the sound of someone moving about in the room. It was Connor.

For some reason, I didn't want to move and let him

know I was awake. I didn't even want to talk to him or face him, but I had to. I had no choice.

Connor was in the closet, trying to take off his clothes and put on new ones. So, I got up, walked to the door of the closet, and leaned on it.

"You're home," I said. Connor turned to me immediately, and the expression on his face hurt me. It was like he didn't want me there. He still didn't want me to see him.

"There's no use trying to avoid me right now. We're going to talk about this, and we'll talk about this right now," I smiled at him.

"Ken, it's not what you think," he said.

"Connor, I really think it's what I think. It's what I think," I scoffed.

"I'm not here to pick a fight with you. I just want you to tell me the truth. Rid me of this hurt I feel in my heart for you and make me trust you without a doubt again. Right now, I'm feeling a lot of things, and it's not in your favor," I told him.

Connor took in a deep breath. Then, he walked toward me, putting his hands on my shoulders.

"I'm sorry," he apologized.

"I'm sorry for acting so cowardly and hurting you in the process. I was embarrassed and scared. I didn't know how to face you," Connor said as he leaned in and put his forehead on mine.

"What does you mean? Don't you trust me? Or love me? Why did we get married if you knew you didn't trust me enough to tell me about the inner battles you're fighting, so we can fight them together?" I asked him.

"It's not as easy as you think, Ken. I did a lot of horrible things. Things I thought I could get away from, but they caught up with me. I tried my best to leave my old life behind, but it caught up with me," Connor's voice shook.

What were the things he was trying to leave behind? Were they the things Rose talked about? Did he really kill people and destroy families?

Chapter fourteen

"Tell me, Connor, what are these things?" I asked him. Connor's head fell; he ran his fingers through his hair and then looked at me through his hair, his head still hanging low.

"Ken, I'm sorry, but I can't say them. The plan was to leave that life behind. I don't want to talk about it and constantly remind myself about it. I really want to tell you, but I can't," Connor's voice was deep and solemn. He couldn't tell me what he did, and why he did it.

"Then tell me about Rose. What's her deal?" I asked him. Connor raised his head, locking his eyes on mine; he walked over to me, grabbed my hand, and led me to the bed to sit. Connor crouched down in front of me while looking up at me.

"Rose brings back so many bad memories. Look, Ken, I love you, and I'm saved, that's all that should matter to you," Connor caressed my hands in his.

Yes, I knew his salvation in Christ was very important, and it was the only thing I should consider now, but I wanted to know everything about him. I wanted to know everything he'd been through before and after his salvation. I married the man, so I had the right to know everything about him. I mean he knows everything I suffered in my last marriage. At some point, he was part of it, and he helped me heal. I wanted to help him heal too, just like he did for me.

"I want to know, Connor. Trying to change the topic won't stop me from asking, it'll only raise suspicions," I told him. Connor took a deep breath and looked around the room like he was looking for something.

"You suspect me?"

"Yes, well, you're not giving me any reason not to. That's why you have to answer my questions. I'll believe you because we're married, and nothing can change that," I caressed his hands.

"So, you won't believe me because you love me, but because we're married?" Connor asked.

"Connor! Just answer my questions! What's the deal with Rose?" I asked. I was getting fed up with his behavior. This was not the Connor I knew.

"Fine. Rose and I were friends; she was like my next-door neighbor, and so we started hanging out. When I got into trouble, she'd always come to help.

Even when I started doing horrible stuff, she joined me because, according to her, she couldn't bear to see me do horrible stuff alone. So, she ran away from home, and we started living together in a broken-down house," Connor started. Friends? Next-door neighbor friends?

"That's all we were. When I decided to leave, she was in too deep and didn't want to leave with me. Rose was broken and gone. There was no bringing her back," Connor continued.

That's all they were? Rose mentioned she was his ex-wife, and Connor was saying they were just friends. Why was he trying to hide the fact that he married Rose from me? What was so horrible that he was trying to hide it?

"What about your ex-wife then?" I asked him. Connor's eyes widened like he had been caught doing something he wasn't supposed to be doing. I was hurt, to say the least.

"Ken..." Connor called.

"I just want to help you, but if you keep lying and hiding stuff from me, I don't think I can help you in any way. I think I'll go stay with Scott, Carol, and the kids for a few days until you're ready to tell me the truth." I pushed Connor's hands from mine, getting up from the bed to leave. I couldn't believe he'd lie to my face.

"Wait, Ken! Please don't go. Don't do this to me. It took me a very long time to leave my old life behind. Even after I was saved, I still had nightmares about everything. The thought of you leaving me right now is messing me up; it's bringing back bad memories, and I don't want that. Ken, please don't go. I'll tell you everything you need to know. I won't keep anything away from you," Connor got up and hugged me, hiding his face in the crook of my neck. I wanted to comfort him – tell him everything would be okay and tell him I wouldn't leave him – but I didn't know how to.

"Ken, I love you, more than is allowed, but I don't think I can bear this alone. I need you, Ken. Please, let me explain," Connor's voice cracked. He was crying.

"Fine, let's talk then. Tell me everything. I'm ready to go through all this with you," I told him. "God please give me the strength to take it." I prayed. If everything Rose said was true, then I needed help from God to take in all that Connor would tell me.

Connor sat me down on the bed, but this time, he sat down beside me, holding my hands in his.

"Before you say anything, Rose came to see me earlier," I told him. Connor froze, but he relaxed a few seconds later.

"Before I say anything, Rose is known for being a professional liar," Connor said with so much venom in his voice. If the situation wasn't so serious, I would've laughed in his face. The way he said it was so cute and funny.

"So?"

"Rose probably told you she's my ex-wife, right?" Connor asked, I nodded my head. How did he know?

"It's not the first time she went about telling people

we were married. She has always had an unhealthy obsession when it comes to me. I tried to push her away, but she did the most horrible things, like try to take her life and stuff," Connor said. It reminded me of Isabella's behaviors.

"I never married her. I never even thought about it. She has a mind of her own," Connor said.

"Tell me what happened then."

Chapter fifteen

"Before I was saved, I used to be a really horrible person. I did the most horrible things to people. I sold drugs, and I was quite popular because I knew how to get people to buy drugs from me, even if they had never taken drugs before. It was serious business, and Jon, the guy who got me into it, really liked me. He liked me so much I was the second in command to everything he had," Connor started.

"I was about twenty-one then, so I more or less knew what I was doing. I got into trouble a lot. I fought a lot. I even ended a couple of lives," he paused to look at me. I took in a deep breath and nodded my head, letting him know it was okay to continue talking.

"Ken, these things I did were very horrible okay, and I can't go into detail," Connor searched my eyes, I complied.

"Three years into drug dealing and the other stuff I did, I met Casey, Jon's sister. She wasn't into drug dealing, but she did other horrible stuff. Jon didn't let her take drugs, but she always found ways to get drugs, especially from me. Casey fancied me a lot, and it was the same for me, I liked her. A few weeks later, Casey and I started dating but in secret. Eventually, Jon found out, but he wasn't as angry as we thought he'd be. He was ecstatic even. After a few months of dating Casey, I really thought she was the one for me, so I asked her to marry me. The wedding was trash, but I didn't care. Rose, on the other hand, cared a lot; she was angry and spiteful. Her anger ended though because she became best friends with Casey," Connor paused.

Rose, best friends with Casey? It was a trick. I knew the likes of Rose and how they behaved. They were sly and would always try to act cool so they could stab from behind.

"Casey liked the idea of being friends with someone who had known me for a very long time. Rose was that person. Casey adored the friendship with Rose, so much that it felt like Casey married Rose and not me. I didn't mind though; I liked the two women being friends because I didn't know what Rose was planning at the time.

Fast forward to seven months into my marriage, Casey started behaving some type of way that wasn't the Casey I knew I liked. She argued about everything, complained about everything, and always tried to pick fights with me for no reason. It was almost like she hated me. Anytime we fought, she'd run to Rose for advice, and only God knows what lies Rose fed her.

From then on, my marriage became very toxic. I couldn't concentrate on work. I was arrested by the police a couple of times, but Jon always bailed me out because he had a very long leg across the city. At some point, he got tired of bailing me and told me if I was caught by the police one more time, he'd let me rot in there. I knew I was on my own then. So, I tried to live a peaceful life, void of Casey and all her drama, but it wasn't as easy as it sounds," Connor had tears threatening to fall from his eyes. The memories were too much to handle.

"I started consuming an unhealthy amount of alcohol and, in one of my drunken states, I slept with Rose. Rose became very vicious and entitled: always coming to my house with the shortest and most revealing clothes. One day, Casey and Rose had a fight when I wasn't home, and when I came back, the duo continued with me. Jon joined the fight and threatened to castrate me. It was pretty serious.

So, I told Rose I wanted nothing to do with her again. I told Casey I wanted a divorce. I told Jon I wanted out, and I never wanted to see any of them again. I took with me the little money I had saved and went into hiding. Jon was angry. He told the policemen under him to find me and tell the other policemen that I was the owner of the cartel and such. Everyone was looking for me, and I almost got caught, but then someone dragged me into a church. He was a pastor, Pastor Carlos; he led me to salvation. He helped bring me out of my dark days. He helped me do the things I never thought I could do, which was to stop taking alcohol and drugs. It took a long while, but we did it.

Pastor Carlos helped me back on my feet and got me a decent job.

At some point, I knew Jon and the crew were after me, but I didn't know they'd be so serious about it, especially after all these years. I thought they had given up on me. I thought I was completely free from that life and everything and everyone that has to do with it," Connor finished. I didn't even know I was crying until Connor wiped my face with his palms. Those horrible people made him the way he was and now that he's better, they still want him?

As people say, what the devil gives will never last, and he'd always come for the lives of those he deceived. Thankfully, Connor was saved, so no devil could claim him, especially when he has me, his praying wife.

"I'm sorry for everything. I'm sorry for being a coward and making you worry so much. I didn't like the thought of you looking at me a different way. I was scared that what I feared the most was coming to bite me in the butt," Connor apologized. I nodded and hugged him tight to me.

"I'm sorry too. I doubted you. I thought about the most horrible things about you. I'm sorry," I apologized.

"I don't want to fight with you ever again, it's not pretty," Connor cozied up to me.

"Me too. Thank you for telling me, at least now we can think about what we can do with God's help," I said as I ran my fingers through his head. Connor nodded.

Chapter sixteen

The smiles on Carol and Scott's faces told me how happy they were to see Connor and me. We had come to take the girls back home with us because the environment at home was back to normal, if not even better.

After Connor told me everything, I understood him better, and it made our relationship with each other even stronger. If it was possible, I loved him even more than I did before. Connor was a good man. Even though his past was horrible, he was born again; he was saved, and he loved me.

"I don't think the girls want to leave anytime soon," Carol smiled sadly at me. She loved Destiny and Kendra so much, and the same was for Scott.

"That much is true. Destiny didn't even ask to facetime you, and you know just how obsessed with you she is," Scott joked. I laughed at the couple. It seemed like they already planned a coup to make us let the girls stay with them.

"Babe, we should let Carol and Scott keep them for one more day. I don't think they're ready to release our children just let," Connor took my hands in his. I looked from Connor to the couple and smiled.

"Okay, they can stay."

"You need all your concentration to prepare your speech for Sunday evening," Scott smiled. Sunday evening's speech?

"Don't tell me you forgot you have a fellowship on Sunday evening?" Scott was bewildered. I was even worse! With everything that had been happening with me and Connor, I totally forgot I had a fellowship on Sunday. Dear Lord! I keep forgetting the most important things.

"What would I do without you, Scott?" Scott laughed.

"At least you have tomorrow, which is Saturday, to get it done," Scott nodded.

"We'll get going now. We need to go prepare that speech truly," Connor laughed, causing Scott and Carol to join in. I rolled my eyes and called out Destiny and Kendra to say bye to them."

"I'll see you, pretty girls, on Sunday," I hugged them.

"Okay mommy, we love you," My girls hugged me back. I could see Carol thanking me for letting them stay till Sunday, from the side of my eyes.

"Bye, daddy," they said and hugged Connor.

"Bye," I said while waving to Carol and Scott, then Connor and I made our way out of their house and into our car.

"I can't believe you forgot about the fellowship," Connor mocked.

"Even I can't believe I forgot about it. I feel so bad. I've not been taking the things of God seriously," I shook my head.

"Come on, don't say that. You have a lot on your mind, and if we had not resolved the matter last night, you wouldn't have come here and then you wouldn't remember at all," Connor said, which only made it worse.

"Gee, thanks," I smiled and rolled my eyes.

"You're good babe, you're good. Everyone knows you don't even need to write your speech, you're that good and smart," Connor complimented. I smiled at his words.

"Thank you, husband," I combed my fingers through his hair. Connor smiled sweetly at me then started the car. As we drove home, there was one thing on my mind.

A marriage backed by God can and will never fail.

When Sunday evening finally came, I was very prepared. I didn't write a speech, instead I spent that time praying. Prayers were more important because I knew God would give me the right words to use to speak to his children.

The fellowship had already started, and the hall was fully packed as usual with mostly women and young ladies. The host led the crowd in prayers; I liked how the whole crowd was fired up, praying and worshiping God.

A sudden urge to pee came and I ran to the ladies' room. When I came out of the toilet, I saw a familiar profile beside me.

"Isabella?" I called. She turned to me with a smile on her face. I was shocked.

"Hi Ken," she waved.

"You got out!" I smiled.

"Not really, a certain someone pulled a few strings to make me attend this fellowship. He said it'll be good for building my faith," Isabella smiled.

He? Who was he? Connor?

"Connor?" I asked.

"Nope, Larry's Uncle, Samuel," she smiled.

"You know, I never really liked the man because he was always against me and Larry, and he loved you so much," Isabella washed her hands.

Samuel was keeping tabs on me? I mean I knew the man has connections everywhere in the world, but he was still bothered about things that happened with me?

"He came to see me one time and told me he had released all the hate he had for me since I decided to repent. He said he felt guilty because his nephew was almost the cause of how I turned out, and he wanted to help me. He begged me to be nice to you," she laughed like she couldn't believe the words Samuel said to her. I could believe those were his words – he was Macho man Uncle Samuel.

"That's like him," I laughed too.

"I'm really looking forward to this fellowship, it's the first time I'm attending one," Isabella smiled and left the ladies' room. I washed my hands and followed after her. I made a mental note to call Samuel later.

"Hey, where have you been?" Connor walked to me when I entered the hall.

"I went to the ladies. Is everything okay?" I asked him.

"It's almost time for you to go up," he said, and I nodded.

"You won't believe who I just saw," I smiled.

"Who?"

"Isabella. She's here for the meeting; that makes me so happy," I smiled toward the aisle I saw Isabella walk to.

"How is she here?"

"And now, let's welcome our one and only women's fellowship speaker, Mrs. Kendall Collins," the host said, and the crowd went wild with clapping and shouting.

"Later," I mouthed to Connor and went toward the stage, smiling at the crowd.

Chapter seventeen

"I'm sure many of you have heard about me and what happened with my first marriage," I spoke loud with the help of the mic I was holding.

"My first marriage was everything a bad marriage could be. It was physically, verbally, and emotionally abusive, all because I couldn't give birth. The man claimed he loved me, but he wanted something I couldn't give him. You might be in this place going through the same thing; I'm telling you now, don't let a man lay his hands on you while you sit and do nothing just because you love him. Someone who loves you would never resort to violence for anything concerning you. Go to God. I'm a living testimony of the grace, favor, and mercy of God," I told the congregation; a lot of women nodded in response.

"After praying to God to take me out of that abusive relationship, God did, and he sent me the best man I have ever come across," I said, and my eyes darted to Connor. He was sitting in front, close to the stage.

"Even if the man is not yours? Are you going to keep deceiving yourself because you think this new man is sent from your God," asked a very loud and angry voice. The congregation was startled, looking back to see where the voice came from.

Rose!

She had somehow managed to be here, and it looked like her plan was to cause confusion, which worked well for her. There were small talks from here and there based on what Rose said.

"Tell them, Ken! Tell them who this good man really is. Is he as good as you make him out to be? Are we going to forget all the harm he has caused? Are you going to ignore the lives he took all because he was sent from God?" Rose yelled.

"Rose!" I yelled in annoyance. She was going too far with this. She had no right to make our private lives public like that, especially at a fellowship.

"Don't Rose me! Tell them who this good man of yours is!"

"Rose! You're taking this too far. Go backstage and we'll talk. It's disrespectful for you to interrupt the people of God at a gathering like this!" I told her.

"So, you do care about your image?" Rose scoffed. My eyes went straight to where Connor sat. He wasn't there anymore.

Oh, dear Lord please take control of this situation.

When I looked back at Rose, who was at the far end of the hall, I saw Connor dragging her away.

"Don't fucking touch me!" Rose yelled, swatting Connor's hands away from her body.

The older women in the congregation gasped at the foul word Rose used.

"Kendall, I told you I wasn't done with you. If you're going to stand before God's people, then at least say the truth! Don't stand there and lie to your heart's content. That makes you a liar, you know, a con artist even!" Rose yelled.

"What do you stand to gain from doing this?" I asked her. Rose laughed.

"Connor belongs to me. I let him off for all these years thinking he'll come to his senses and do the right thing, but then he goes around and gets married to you? Where does that fucking leave me? Huh? I have always been there for him. I did everything for him. I was there during his dark days when he'd shoot people until they took their last breath! I'm the one who helped him fight his demons, so you can't just stand there and claim him to be your good man sent from God. I won't take that shit! Not from you or even from you," Rose yelled.

"Stop this Rose! You're making a fool of yourself. What in heaven happened to you?" Connor yelled. That was the loudest I had ever heard Connor's voice; it was almost like he had a microphone with him, and he didn't.

"You! You happened to me! You refused to love me when I gave you my heart, and now you want to complain about the way I turned out? It's your fault, so come and take responsibility for what you did to me!!!" Rose yelled at Connor. As I stood there, watching Rose and Connor argue back and forth with each other, my heart broke. This was the same thing with Larry and Isabella, only there was a Rose in Connor's life before I came in.

Hot tears spilled from my eyes as I watched them argue. I was so glad my life got better, and I didn't have an abusive husband again, but what was going on was emotionally abusive, and I didn't know what I could do to stop it. Were abusive relationships bound to find me no matter what? What did I do to always go through this? This was not the plan God had for me. I was never meant to suffer this much. This was the devil trying to make me miserable.

The microphone I held fell from my hands to the ground; I covered my face with my hands to block my tears from prying eyes as I ran off of the stage.

Rose was truly evil. I couldn't believe she'd do such a thing.

"Rose!" A foreign voice called. I knew that voice all too well.

Isabella?

I turned to the stage to find Isabella on the stage with the microphone I had dropped in her hands. Everyone in the congregation had their attention on the newcomer.

"I usually don't help people or do this type of stuff, but someone told me to be nice to Kendall," Isabella winked at me.

"Rose, what you're going through right now, I have gone through it. I was the one who caused most of the problems Ken faced in her first marriage," Isabella said. The congregation gasped at Isabella's sudden confession; even I was shocked. What did Isabella think she was trying to do? I kept my eyes on her, trying to figure out what was going on in her head, but I got nothing.

Chapter eighteen

"Ken's ex-husband had come to me asking me to be a surrogate for them since Ken couldn't conceive. Of course, it was supposed to be a surprise for Ken. That was his plan, but I spoiled that plan with my stupid feelings. I felt like I was giving him what he wanted, what his wife couldn't give him, so he should be with me and not her. The man got distracted and started spending more time with me than with the woman he married. I liked that he was rich, and he could provide everything I had lost and couldn't have as a child. I liked the security the man provided. I was blinded by greed." As Isabella spoke, more tears formed, and I let them out freely.

"Ken didn't deserve what I did to her. She didn't even know my deal; she didn't know about her ex-husband's plans to give her a child. This man became really hateful toward Ken, and I was happy he was giving me more attention and money than he was doing with Ken. I knew Ken wanted nothing to do with us after she found out about us. She found a way to leave the man; she got a restraining order and all. It was very serious.

Her ex-husband became sick and decided he wanted to give everything he had to Ken and the baby I later gave birth to. I was angry, boiling with rage. I had done all this man wanted me to do, and he wanted to give all my hard work to the woman who left him, who left everything behind? I got too angry and shot him. When the police started looking for me, I killed my twin sister and put her in a tub to pose as me, so I was declared dead. I was depressed, angry, and all alone." Some people in the congregation were shedding tears at Isabella's story.

"Look, I was horrible, and I never thought redemption was impossible. I tried to kill Ken twice, but she never died. Ken looked me in the eyes while I had a gun to her face and told me she wasn't going to die. She had faith in God, something I thought was a useless belief." The congregation went wild with claps and howls. While some couldn't believe their ears.

"After everything I did to Ken, including kidnapping her children and threatening to kill them with you, Rose, I couldn't do it. Not because I didn't want to, but because something held me back. I felt trapped, like I was attacked by some strong force and I couldn't move. Ken, I never told you this, but I was only able to move when you arrived," Isabella smiled at me.

"Why did I tell this story? It's because you're trying to repeat history Rose, and this war won't be in your favor. I tried Ken and her God, look where it brought me, on stage talking to a bunch of people I don't know," Isabella wiped her face with the hem of her shirt. She took in a deep breath and continued talking.

Of all the reasons God wanted me to help save Isabella, I never thought it would be because she'd be the one to save me from shame and everything else.

"If you don't want to come to God and be saved, that's on you, but you shouldn't mess with God, especially when it comes to Ken and her family," I smiled at Isabella's words.

"Of all the things I've learned about being saved is that they call it born again for a reason. It means all the sins you committed in your past life would be cleared, and you're being offered a new life in Christ. You're a new man. I killed my sister when I was in the world. I thought she would always haunt me, but when I came to God, I had good dreams about her. I never for once had any more nightmares. It must be the same with Connor. He may have done those things while he was in the world before he was saved. Now, he knows better. God would never give a bad man to Ken anymore. Or do any one of you think God will give a bad and unsaved man to Ken?" Isabella asked and the congregation yelled "no" in unison.

I was a crying mess in the corner.

"So, what's it going to be Rose? Are you going to keep going after the version of Connor you knew, who is now dead, or are you going to give up?" Isabella asked her. The congregation turned to Rose. She looked like she was ashamed of herself for being there.

"You're delusional! If I knew this was the reason why you threw me under the bus, I would've killed you that day," Rose spat.

"Yes, perhaps you could've done that then, but now you can't. It's too late at this point because I can't die!" Isabella smirked, gaining praises from the congregation for her bravery.

"Go home, Rose. When God arrests you, you'd either come back here or you'd meet me in jail, either way, you'll be saved," Isabella added. I almost forgot that Isabella was only out for a fellowship. I smiled at Isabella's words as my legs carried me to the stage.

I hugged Isabella tightly. She had done for me what I couldn't do. God used her to help Connor and I out of shame.

"Thank you, sister, I'll forever be grateful to you for today," I told her.

"No need to. I didn't do it for you to be indebted to me, no, I did it because I had a move in my spirit. I thought it was the right thing to do," Isabella smiled at me. The congregation clapped for us. They were filled with excitement.

Isabella and I watched Rose as she rolled her eyes at us. Connor had a sad smile on his eyes. I smiled back at him, telling him it was all good and we'd be fine.

"Go to your man," Isabella nudged me. I giggled

shyly and did as she said. When I got to Connor, he opened his arms wide for me, I fit myself into the space, hugging him as he did the same.

"I love you," we said at the same time.

"Well, let's see if this your God will save you now!" Rose smirked and pulled out a black gun from her purse. The congregation became wild as everyone tried to get away from any bullet that may fly.

"Rose…" Isabella started to say, but a gunshot was fired. Isabella was on the floor with her hand on her stomach.

"You're up next," Rose smiled, pointing her gun toward Connor and I, but her eyes were locked on me.

God help us.

I shut my eyes tight and I prayed. I felt the weight of Connor's body on mine before I heard the gunshot.

"I love you."

Epilogue

A marriage backed by God will never fail.

I started believing those words after my final separation from Larry. It felt like the truest thing. After I heard it, it was like throughout the years I stayed married to him, I was living a lie. Like God wasn't happy with me because I was married to a man who wasn't for me.

When I was younger, I had met Larry. I thought he was everything a good man should be. He was calm, kind, loving, and always had me in mind. He always tried to make me comfortable. He did things men don't usually do anymore. He bought me gifts and all, so I thought I got a good man. When we got married, all these things didn't stop; he kept doing them until he found out I couldn't give birth. I had miscarried all the children in my womb. At first, he wasn't bothered by the first two miscarriages. It was after it became a serious thing that we started having problems.

That was the test God gave to Larry, to prove his said "love" for me, and he failed it. All Larry wanted was a child and a stay-at-home mother to cater child's needs because he had told me he was never going to let me work.

That was the life Larry envisioned for himself. The only thing lacking was that Larry never loved me as much as he claimed he did.

Which was why when I got a taste of real love from Connor, even I could tell it was real. Not because he was pretty to look at, or because he was doing things for me, no. It was because he saw me; he saw me, and he loved me regardless.

He had seen me suffer in New York. He saw how messy my life was, yet he looked me in the face and said he wasn't going anywhere. He was going to stay with me to prove to me that his love for me was not based on my looks. He loved me for me and loved everyone around me, including my children that weren't biologically his. Connor loved us regardless, and that's what true love is.

A marriage backed by God will never fail, and that was my testimony.

About the Author

Erica T Capri is the bestselling author behind the "A Thin Line" Trilogy series. She finds pleasure in writing fiction, non-fiction, romance, children's literature, articles, self-help books, and so much more.

Erica is a stylist, an entrepreneur, a film producer as well as a playwright. Her work as a playwright has become popular over the years with her production performing at Colleges and theatre stages.

Altogether, Erica has written over twenty pieces in the combination of stage plays, screenplays, and novels. She has coached over 20 authors and has ghostwritten more than 15 projects being the COO of Gemlight Publishing company.

Erica's life goals are simple -- she's big on family and self-care, so when she's not writing, she's taking care of her two beautiful young children.

Erica T Capri has no plans to stop writing anytime soon and is hard at work on her book and film releases.

Read Erica's Books in Order!

Book 1: No Trouble Today

Book 2: Prayers For The Prey: The Escape Plan to Overcoming Sexual Abuse

> ### *A Thin Line Series*
>
> *Book 3:* A Thin Line Between Love and Obsession
>
> *Book 4:* A Thin Line Between Love & Fear
>
> *Book 5:* A Thin Line Between Love and Revenge

Join Erica's mailing list at **www.ericacapri.com** for updates on her new releases and free e-books. Follow her on Instagram at **@erica_capriwriter**

ERICA_CAPRIWRITER

GEMLIGHTPUBLISHING

www.ingramcontent.com/pod-product-compliance
Lightning Source LLC
Chambersburg PA
CBHW030215130726
47898CB00012B/1029